GRASPER

A YOUNG CRAB'S DISCOVERY

*For the students of Central Park school......
May you each discover your very
own LARGER WORLD,
within and without!*

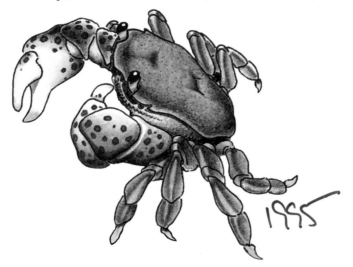

1995

BEYOND WORDS PUBLISHING, INC.

Paul Owen Lewis

WRITTEN AND ILLUSTRATED BY
PAUL OWEN LEWIS

Published by

Beyond Words Publishing, Inc.

13950 NW Pumpkin Ridge Road

Hillsboro, Oregon 97124

Phone: 503-647-5109

To order: 1-800-284-9673

Design: Principia Graphica

Printed in Canada

Distributed by Publishers Group West

ISBN: 0-941831-85-X 14.95 hard cover

Library of Congress Cataloging–in–Publication Data

Lewis, Paul Owen.
    Grasper: a young crab's discovery out of his shell /
written and illustrated by Paul Owen Lewis.
        p. cm.
    Summary: Grasper the crab gains self-confidence
after exploring the world outside his tide pool.
    ISBN 0-941831-85-X : $14.95
    [1. Crabs--Fiction. 2. Self-confidence--Fiction.]
    I. Title.
PZ7.L58765Gr 1993
[Fic}--dc20   93-18383
                                       CIP
                                        AC

OTHER BOOKS BY PAUL OWEN LEWIS

EVER WONDERED? For Explorers, Inventors
                          and Artists of All Ages
DAVY'S DREAM: A Young Boy's Adventure
                          with Wild Orca Whales
P. BEAR'S NEW YEAR'S PARTY: A Counting Book
THE STARLIGHT BRIDE

For Marie,

whose heart
is always soft.

Grasper lived
deep between the rocks
beside the sea,
where he spent his days
looking for bits of food
drifting in with the tide.

But, with so many others
there looking too,
a scrap of seaweed
or nibble of dead fish
was all he could hope to find.

When one day...

Grasper began to feel quite peculiar, almost swollen inside, like he was having a stomach ache. Only he felt this way through his entire body.

"I feel as if I'm going to burst!" exclaimed the little crab.

And he was. Like taking off a coat, now too small for him, Grasper's shell split open along his back, and before he knew it, he had crawled backwards outside himself—or at least what used to be himself. There in front of him was his whole shell: his body, legs, claws and even his eyes!

The other crabs in the pool saw this and came running. Surrounding Grasper, they asked,

"How do you feel?"

"I can hardly move!" cried Grasper, "but I *feel* wonderful, like a new crab.

What's happened to me?"

"Of course you can hardly move," said one, "you've just molted for the first time, and your new shell hasn't hardened yet to help you."

"Of course you *feel* wonderful," said another, "when a crab's out of his shell, he's out of his mind too!"

"And that's dangerous," said a third, "since a crab must have both a hard shell and a hard heart to survive. Be careful until your new shell has hardened Grasper, and don't listen to any new thoughts you might have."

"You're going to feel like walking out in the open on your new legs."

"You're going to want to see what's over the top of the rocks with your new eyes."

"You're even going to believe there are better things to eat there with your new mouth!" warned others in the circle.

"You mean this has happened to all of you too?" Grasper asked.

"Of course! many times!" they shouted.

But Grasper couldn't help it. Some time later, he began to ask himself, "Could there be another world out there? What will I see over the top of the rocks? Maybe there *are* better things to eat out there!"

Now, he really was having the thoughts they had warned him about.

Feeling some strength return to his legs, Grasper began to scramble out from under the rocks. The other crabs ran to block his path.

"Don't do it!" shouted one, "these thoughts will pass!"

"Stay here with us!" shouted another. "It isn't safe out there!"

The little crab began to climb.

"GRASPER STOP!" they cried. "NO ONE HAS EVER RETURNED!"

There *was* a whole world out there!

He set off to explore, and he found...

...a large fish,

...a shiny treasure,

...a hungry seagull,

...and a giant!

"What are you looking at?" asked the huge crab.

"You! You're so s...so big!" stuttered Grasper.

"Of course I am!" boomed the giant. "And you will be too, after you've molted as many times as I have."

"Me...as big as you?" cried Grasper. "But how? Where I come from...under the rocks...there are other crabs who've molted many times—but they haven't grown larger."

"Do they never leave these rocks of yours?" he asked.

"No, they are afraid to," replied Grasper.

"Well, then of course!" said the crab. "Everyone knows a crab will only grow as large as the world he lives in, and as big as the heart inside him.

You must have a big heart to live in a big world."

"But they told me I must have a hard heart, not a big heart," said Grasper.

"A hard heart will not grow, little one. And," he continued, "if you're not careful to let your heart grow on the inside of you, neither will your shell grow around it on the outside of you—no matter how many times you shed it."

"Then a soft heart isn't dangerous?" asked Grasper.

"Oh yes, it can be," he replied, "but it is the only way a crab can really grow."

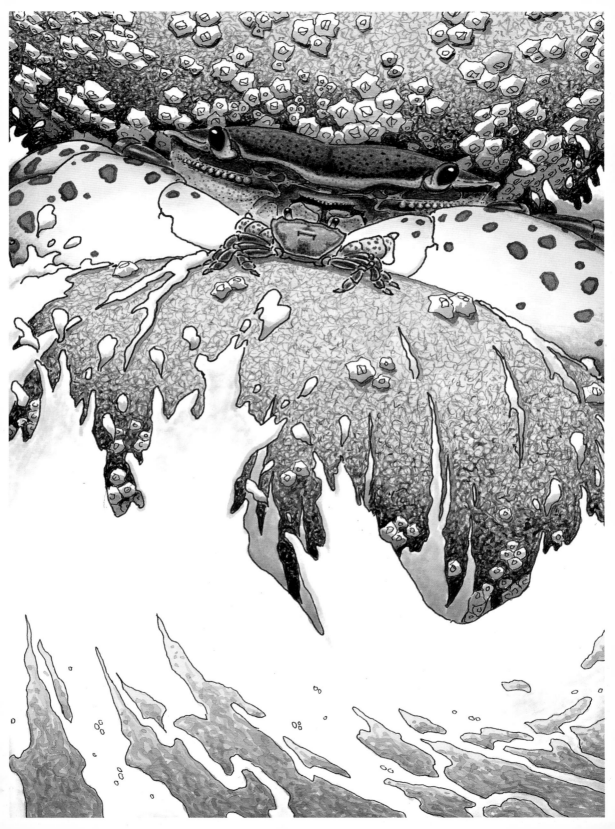

Although Grasper had never heard such things before,
he knew that
**what the giant crab
had told him was true.**

He felt he must tell the others, and carefully he set off to find them again.

"Look!" someone cried, "isn't that Grasper?"

"He looks bigger," said another.

The little crabs quickly surrounded Grasper and asked, "What did you see?"

Excitedly Grasper began to tell them about the world beyond the safety of their rocks; the colors, the food, the fish, the treasure, the seagull, the wave, the giant crab and what he had said. But, as he spoke, the little crabs in the circle took their eyes off him, one by one. Most looked at each other. Some looked down and stirred the sand slowly with their claws. Then, before he could finish, one of them broke in and said, "Colors and treasures! Giant crabs, indeed!"

Grasper stopped speaking. For a moment, no one said anything. No one would look at him.

"You don't believe me do you?"

Grasper demanded.

"Of course we do," said one. "A crab is likely to imagine many things when he is soft. After all, it's only natural when you're frightened. Why, the last time I was soft, I thought I saw a creature as tall as the sky, walking on only two legs."

"I once thought I saw a fish as big as the sea that blew air and water out of its head!" exclaimed another.

The little circle erupted with laughter.

"See Grasper," said another, "stay here with us and give your shell time to harden completely. Once it does, you won't imagine those things anymore. You'll forget them and be safe again."

"But I'm sure I saw..." Grasper began to say. But something strange was beginning to happen; he couldn't remember clearly. Instead he said, "That's funny...now that I'm down here again, those things don't seem so real.

Maybe I did imagine it after all."

"Of course you did," said one.
"Of course I did," repeated Grasper.
"It's only natural!" reminded another.
"It's only natural," Grasper repeated softly.
Grasper was staring blankly at the sand in front of him. The colors, the treasure, even the giant crab, faded from his mind.

His shell had hardened completely.

Grasper passed his time like the others now, clawing through the sand for things to eat, when one day, a huge shadow passed over him. Grasper looked up and his eyes opened wide! A large fish was swimming over the rocks—just like one who had tried to eat him!

"I didn't imagine that fish!" cried Grasper.

Suddenly, he could remember again! And, he began to feel quite peculiar, almost swollen inside, like he was having a stomach ache through his entire body. Then,

CRACK!

Grasper's hardened shell split open and he was outside of it once again. His heart felt free and soft once more!

Quickly, Grasper stumbled to climb up the rocks as best he could on his soft new legs. A few of the other little crabs followed him, scrambling to block his path, but it was too late. Grasper reached the top—and so did the others.

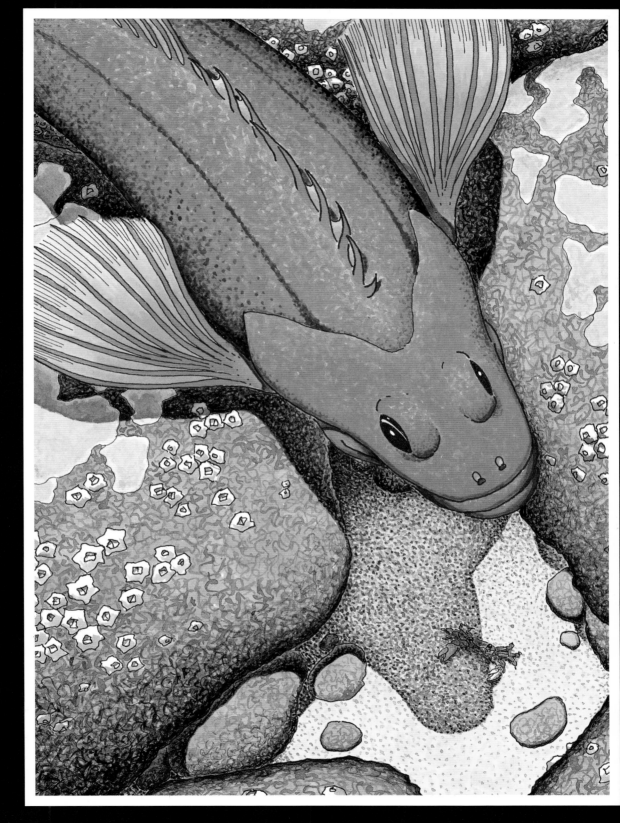

"Oh my!" said one. "It's beautiful," said a second.
"Grasper, you didn't imagine it!" said a third.

Grasper and his friends left their little world between the rocks that day.
And...they never returned.

Other Story Books by Beyond Words

THE MAYBE GARDEN
Author: Kimberly Burke-Weiner, Illustrator: Fredrika Spillman, $14.95 hardbound, $7.95 softbound

A beautiful, poetic story about a young child's quest to become an independent and creative thinker. The child uses Mother's ordinary suggestions for a garden as a springboard for unique and original ideas. Through the child's creativity, the spirit of the rest of the neighborhood is also sparked and the magic blooms in other gardens. The wildly colorful illustrations will capture the imaginations of young readers, while the fanciful text plants ideas in their heads. A humorous surprise ending will challenge the stereotypes of both adult and child. Ages 3-10.

GROWING WILD: Inviting Wildlife Into Your Yard
Author/Illustrator: Constance Perenyi, $14.95 hardbound, $9.95 softbound

A children's book charmingly illustrated with four-color images crafted of cut and torn paper, and printed on high quality recycled paper. The story chronicles the changes of a suburban neighborhood from biologically depleted plots of lawn to a living, diverse environment. With pages at the back of the book which explain the gardening/ecological principles in the story, this book introduces young readers to the concept of gardening for wildlife. Easy ideas for parents and children to set up their own wildlife garden. Ages 6-9.

COYOTE STORIES FOR CHILDREN: Tales from Native America
Author: Susan Strauss; Illustrator: Gary Lund, $10.95 hardbound, $6.95 softbound

Storyteller and author Susan Strauss has interspersed Native American coyote tales with true-life anecdotes about coyotes and Native wisdom. This cycle, or small "saga", of coyote's adventures during "the time before the coming of the human beings", illustrates the creative and foolish nature of this popular trickster, and demonstrates the wisdom in Native American humor. Whimsical illustrations weave through the text. Ages 6-12.

CEREMONY IN THE CIRCLE OF LIFE
Author: "White Deer of Autumn"; Illustrator: Daniel San Souci, $14.95 hardbound $6.95 softbound

The story of nine year old "Little Turtle", a young Native American boy growing up in the city without a knowledge of his ancestors' beliefs. He is visited by "Star Spirit", a traveller from the Seven Dancing Stars, who introduces him to his heritage and his relationship to all things in the circle of life. The symbol of the four directions in the wheel of life is explained and illustrated as an important aspect in Native American culture. Little Turtle also learns about nature and how he can help to heal the Earth. Ages 6-10.

THE GREAT CHANGE
Author: "White Deer of Autumn"; Illustrator: Carol Grigg, $13.95 hardbound

A Native American tale in which a wise grandmother explains the meaning of death, or the Great Change, to her questioning granddaughter. Eight year old Wan-Ba asks "Why does the caterpillar have to die? Why did grandfather have to die?" Grandmother explains that just as the caterpillar "dies" only to become a beautiful butterfly, there is no "death" in the Circle of Life, only the Great Change. This is a story of passing on tradition, culture, and wisdom to the next generation. It is a moving tale for everyone who wonders about what lies beyond this life. Watercolor illustrations by internationally acclaimed painter, Carol Grigg, throughout. All ages.

These and other childrens and adult books are available from Beyond Words Publishing
Our mission: "Inspire to Integrity".